Bluebell Woods

Honey's Summer Ball

For Arabella Shepperd
- a real book and animal lover.
L.N.

To the Aunties, Jennifer
and Hilary, with love X
R.H.

STRIPES PUBLISHING
An imprint of Magi Publications
1 The Coda Centre, 189 Munster Road,
London SW6 6AW

A paperback original
First published in Great Britain in 2011

ISBN: 978-1-84715-189-6

A CIP catalogue record for this book is available
from the British Library.

Printed and bound in China.

STP/1800/0002/0311

10 9 8 7 6 5 4 3 2 1

Bluebell Woods

Honey's Summer Ball

Liss Norton

Illustrated by Rebecca Harry

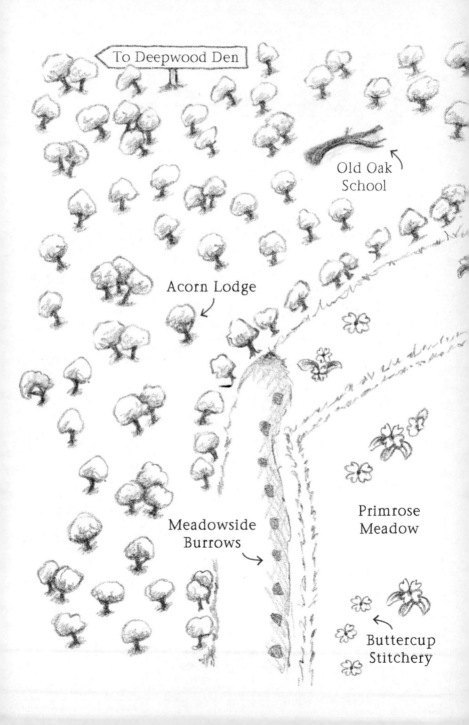

To Deepwood Den

Old Oak
School

Acorn Lodge

Meadowside
Burrows

Primrose
Meadow

Buttercup
Stitchery

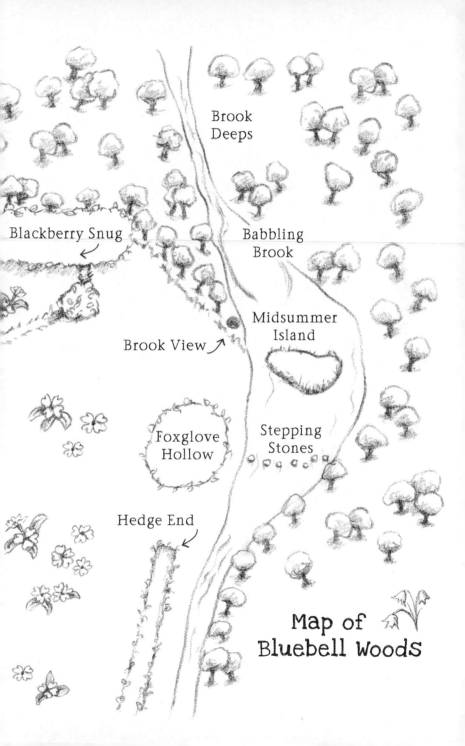

Brook
Deeps

Blackberry Snug

Babbling
Brook

Brook View ↗

Midsummer
Island

Foxglove
Hollow

Stepping
Stones

Hedge End

Map of
Bluebell Woods

Chapter One

It was a beautiful summer's day and Honey
Pennyroyal and her family were enjoying a
picnic breakfast in Primrose Meadow.

"What a shame there's school today!"
Honey sighed. "It's too nice to be indoors."

"Too right!" agreed her brother
Harvey. He flicked a sunflower seed husk
at her, which missed by a whisker.

"Stop that, Harvey," warned Mr
Pennyroyal.

Just then, Honey heard rustling in the
hedgerow behind them, and Mr Chervil the

postman appeared, carrying a bulging sack.

"Oh!" Honey squeaked, leaping up excitedly. "Have you got—?"

"Letters from the Summer Ball committee," said Mr Chervil, winking at Mrs Pennyroyal.

"You're on that committee, aren't you, Mum?" Honey said. "All those planning meetings you've been going to." She watched hopefully as Mr Chervil gave an envelope to her older sister, Hattie, and another to her brother Albie. She'd never been to the Summer Ball before, but this year she was finally old enough.

"I am," said Mrs Pennyroyal.

"Is there one for—?"

"Wait and see," her mum said, smiling.

Mr Chervil handed envelopes to Albie's twin, Harvey, and to her parents.

"One left," he said. "And it's for…" He squinted at the name on the front.

"For me?" Honey cried.

"I believe it is," said Mr Chervil.

With trembling paws, Honey took the envelope. Her name was written in beautiful, swirly writing. She took out the card inside. "'The Summer Ball committee invites Miss Honey Pennyroyal to the Summer Ball on Midsummer Island on 24th June'," she read.

She skipped round in a circle, her tail twitching excitedly. "I'm going to the ball!" she sang. "I'm really, truly going to the ball!"

"I wish I wasn't," Albie groaned.

"And me," agreed Harvey, scowling. "I hate the ball. Dressing up in silly clothes!"

"Walking with girls in the Grand Procession!" added Albie.

"There's nothing wrong with girls," Honey said hotly.

"You're both going," Mr Pennyroyal said firmly. "And that's final."

At that moment, Honey's friends Florence Candytuft, a rabbit, and Evie Morningdew, a squirrel, came dashing across Primrose Meadow. Honey raced to meet them, waving her invitation. "I'm going to the Summer Ball!" she squeaked.

"Me too!" Florence and Evie cried together.

"We should see if Nat's been invited," Evie added. Their friend Natalie Hollyhock, a hedgehog, lived close by the school, in a nest called Blackberry Snug.

"Hang on," Honey said. She scurried back to the picnic blanket to pick up her school bag. "See you later," she called to her family, as she, Florence and Evie set off for Natalie's nest.

"Mrs Buttercup's making Evie's ball dress," said Florence, as they crossed Primrose Meadow. Mrs Buttercup, a badger, was the Bluebell Woods seamstress.

"You lucky thing!" Honey exclaimed. "I'd love to have a dress made, but I'll probably have to wear Hattie's old one."

"Never mind," said Florence. "It'll be brilliant whatever we're wearing."

Honey picked a blade of grass. "If I could choose, I'd have a green dress to match this grass. What colour will you pick, Evie?"

"I haven't decided yet. Mum wants me to go to Mrs Buttercup's after school and choose. Do you want to come?"

"You bet!" Honey and Florence exclaimed.

They reached the edge of Bluebell Woods where a sweet-scented dog rose was flowering. "Or maybe I'd have pale pink," Honey said. "Like that rose.

But I always wear pink… I should probably pick something different. What about blue to match the bluebells?" Only a few of the bluebells that gave Bluebell Woods its name were still in flower.

Evie and Florence laughed. "It's lucky you're not having a new dress," Florence said. "You'd never be able to decide on the colour!"

Natalie's nest was in a bramble thicket on the edge of Bluebell Woods. She was waiting for her friends outside Blackberry Snug.

"Guess what?" Natalie cried.

"The Summer Ball?" Honey said. "We've been invited, too." She grabbed Natalie's paws and swung her round in a circle. "Only two weeks to wait!"

Old Oak School was buzzing with the news of the ball when Honey and her friends reached the playground, a clearing deep in leaf mould and edged with trees. The older pupils, who'd been to the ball before, were chattering excitedly about the dancing, food and decorations. Honey, Evie, Natalie and Florence went over to listen in, but then Mr Hazelgrove and Mrs Wintergreen came out into the playground.

"Classes, please."

Mrs Wintergreen taught the older pupils while Honey, Florence, Natalie and Evie were in Mr Hazelgrove's class. They scurried inside and sat down.

"As I'm sure you know, the Summer Ball is only two weeks away," said Mr Hazelgrove, following them inside. "The squirrels and mice will be hanging lights and decorations, the shrews and otters will prepare Midsummer Island, and everyone else will provide the food. This year the Summer Ball committee has asked our school to organize the entertainment and to help make decorations."

A ripple of anticipation ran round the class. Honey and her friends exchanged excited glances.

"The entertainment will be a dance at Foxglove Hollow, performed by those pupils old enough to have been invited, of course. You will join Mrs Wintergreen's class for this, and she will teach you the dance. And the ball will open with the traditional Midsummer Poem. Who'd like to audition to recite it?"

Honey shot up her paw. There was nothing she liked better than performing.

 She looked around the room, checking who else wanted to do it. Monty Hornbeam and Luke Willowherb both had their paws up.

Mr Hazelgrove handed the three of them copies of the Midsummer Poem. "Practise the first verse for tomorrow," he said. "Of course, it won't only be you three auditioning. I'm sure some of Mrs Wintergreen's class will want to try out, too."

Not too many, I hope, Honey thought. She read through the poem eagerly. It would be a real honour to be picked for such a special role. The only problem was making sure Mr Hazelgrove and Mrs Wintergreen chose her.

Chapter
Two

Straight after school, the four friends
raced round to Mrs Buttercup's workshop,
Buttercup Stitchery. It was crowded with
animals choosing silk and patterns for ball
dresses. Mrs Buttercup was measuring Mrs
Willowherb while her assistant, Jemima, a
young dormouse, was busily sewing at a
table near the window.

Evie browsed along the row of
colourful spider silks. "This would suit
you," Natalie said, pointing to an emerald
green fabric.

Evie held the soft silk to her cheek. "What do you think?" she asked Honey and Florence.

"It looks great against your red fur," said Florence.

Honey looked up from practising the Midsummer Poem. "Lovely," she said. "Oh, I wish I could have a new dress! What are you two wearing?" she asked Florence and Natalie.

"My party dress," replied Florence. "You know, the purple one I got for my birthday."

"I'm wearing my party dress, too," Natalie said. "Mum's adding some lace to the bottom, but I don't want it too long in case I trip over it in the dance. You know what I'm like at dancing!"

"We've got two weeks to practise,"
Florence reminded her. "I'm sure you'll
be fine."

"The pattern book's free!" cried Evie,
darting across the room. Florence, Natalie
and Honey followed her, squeezing
through the crowd. Evie grabbed the
heavy book and sat down in a vacant
chair. She turned the pages slowly.

"That's nice," said Honey, pointing to a high-waisted dress with a full skirt.

"No." Evie turned more pages. "There! That one!" It had puffed sleeves and a wide sash. "The sash can be silver."

On the way home, they spotted Harvey and Albie whispering together behind a tree root. "I bet they're up to something," tutted Honey.

The friends crept closer, keeping under low-growing bushes so they wouldn't be spotted.

At last they were close enough to hear what Harvey and Albie were saying. "We need to come up with something really special for the ball," said Harvey in a low voice. "A fantastic trick!"

20

"I knew it!" whispered Honey. "They're probably planning to play a trick on *me*."

"Someone's under that bush," Albie said. "I heard them whispering."

Linking arms, the four friends stepped out of their hiding place. "You're up to something," said Honey. "And we're going to find out what."

"No chance!" hooted Harvey. The boys ran off into the woods, laughing.

"Why do they always have to spoil everything?" Honey sighed.

Natalie put her arm round her. "Try not to worry about them," she said gently.

"Shall we come back to your house to help you practise the poem?" Evie suggested.

"Yes, please," cried Honey.

At Honey's house they found Mrs Pennyroyal writing a list at the kitchen table. "Oh, Natalie," she said, "that's handy. Can you take this list home for your mum later? She's in charge of the food for the ball, and this will show her who's making what."

Natalie put the slip of paper in her bag, and followed her friends into Honey's room.

Honey read out the first verse of the poem:

> *"Midsummer's Day, a special day*
> *Of joy and jubilation.*
> *Come to the ball. Come one, come all,*
> *And join the celebration!"*

She wrinkled her nose. "Was it loud enough?" she asked.

"Definitely," said Evie. "My ears are still ringing."

They all laughed. "It was really good, Honey," said Florence. "If you do it like that tomorrow, you're bound to be picked."

"I'll just go over it again," Honey said.

By the time she'd recited the verse for the twelfth time, Evie had had enough. "Surely you don't need any more practice, Honey?" she said.

"Well, you know what they say: practice makes per—"

Just then, they heard footsteps pattering along the hall. Evie threw open the bedroom door, just as Honey's older sister walked past. "Will you come and tell us about the ball, please, Hattie?" she begged.

"Oh yes!" cried Honey, the poem forgotten.

"Of course!" Hattie came in and sat on Honey's bed. "We start at Foxglove Hollow on the night of the ball," she said. "It'll be decorated with lanterns. Then someone recites the Midsummer Poem."

"Me, fingers crossed!" squeaked Honey.

"After that, we'll do our dance," Hattie continued. "Then there's the Grand Procession when we parade round the outside of Foxglove Hollow, with the grown-ups joining on behind, and down to Mr Willowherb's raft. He'll take us across the Babbling Brook to Midsummer Island."

"I've never been to Midsummer Island," gasped Evie.

"Then it's all music, dancing and food," Hattie said.

"Mum brought me home a scrummy honey cake last year," said Natalie.

"You brought one for me," said Honey. "Do you remember, Hattie?"

Hattie nodded.

"I wish we didn't have to wait so long," Florence groaned.

There was a knock at the door, and Mrs Pennyroyal came in with a pile of clean clothes. "What will I wear to the ball, Mum?" asked Honey.

"You can have Hattie's old ball dress," she replied. "Why don't you get it out, Hattie? You're wearing your new party dress, aren't you?"

25

Hattie led the way to her bedroom and took the ball dress out of her wardrobe. It had once been blue, but the silk had faded to a dull bluey-grey.

"Oh," Honey said, trying to hide her disappointment. "Thanks, Hattie." She changed into the dress and Natalie buttoned it up.

"It fits perfectly," Hattie said.

Honey nodded glumly. "Yes. Shame it's not brighter."

"The style suits you, though," said Evie.

Honey sighed. "I'm sure it'll be fine," she said, forcing a smile.

"I'll make you a flower necklace," said Natalie. "That'll brighten it up."

"Thanks, Nat."

"Tea's ready," called Mrs Pennyroyal from the kitchen.

"We should go," said Evie. "See you tomorrow, Honey."

"Poor Honey," Florence said to Natalie and Evie, as they crossed Primrose Meadow. "She's putting on a brave face, but she doesn't like her ball dress at all."

"Everyone going to the ball should head outside and join Mrs Wintergreen's class for the dance," said Mr Hazelgrove at school the next day. "The rest of you will make decorations."

The friends skipped outside eagerly. Mrs Wintergreen and the older pupils were already there, and Honey waved to Hattie.

"These are our musicians, who've kindly come along to help us rehearse," said Mrs Wintergreen. Mrs Willowherb had her reed pipe and Mr Wintergreen was holding a drum. "The reed pipe orchestra will play on the night of the ball, of course," she went on, "but two musicians are plenty for rehearsals."

The musicians began to play a cheerful tune. "That is what we'll be dancing to," Mrs Wintergreen said when they'd finished. "Now, form two lines. Boys behind, girls in front."

Everyone lined up. "Good. When the music starts, the girls take four skips forward. Then the boys copy."

The musicians began to play and the girls skipped forward.

"If it's all as easy as this, I'll be OK," Natalie whispered, as they turned to watch the boys skipping after them. Harvey and Albie were in the middle of the boys' line, looking sulky. Instead of skipping, they stomped forward.

"No, no, no!" cried Mrs Wintergreen. "Skipping, boys, not stamping."

They learned more steps: a twirl, four side skips, another twirl, a jump.

"I wish we had dancing lessons every day!" Florence said.

"Me, too," agreed Honey.

"Now, we're going to work with partners," said Mrs Wintergreen when they'd gone through the first half of the dance. "Girls, you will dance with the boy directly behind you in the line."

"Hope I don't get Harvey or Albie," Honey said. She breathed a sigh of relief when she realized that her partner was Monty Hornbeam, a shrew.

"I'm with you, Florence," said Luke Willowherb, an otter.

Natalie and Evie both had to dance

with Albie because there was one extra girl. "Just my luck!" he groaned.

"You're luckier than me!" Harvey exclaimed. "I've got Hattie!"

They practised until it was time for the auditions. "Here goes!" squeaked Honey, scurrying into the classroom.

Both classes crammed into Mr Hazelgrove's classroom to watch. The friends sat at the back.

"She was good," Honey whispered, as Tamsin Clover, a friend of Hattie's, finished reading. She sighed. "Some of the others have been amazing, too. I don't know if I can beat them."

"Just do your best," said Natalie, squeezing her paw.

Honey's turn came at last. She stood up shakily. "Good luck," her friends chorused.

She made her way to the front, then cleared her throat nervously before reading the first verse in a loud, clear voice.

"Thank you, Honey. That's the end of the auditions," announced Mr Hazelgrove. "Go out to play while Mrs Wintergreen and I decide who to pick."

They ran outside, glad of an extra playtime. "How did I do?" asked Honey.

"Great," Florence said. "We could hear every word."

Peeping in at the window, they saw the two teachers sitting at Mr Hazelgrove's desk, talking.

"I wish they'd hurry up and decide," Honey groaned.

"Let's skip," suggested Florence, but just as she got out her skipping rope, Mrs Wintergreen called them back inside.

Honey rushed into the classroom, followed by her friends. She waited anxiously for everyone to sit down.

"The Midsummer Poem will be recited by Honey Pennyroyal," announced Mr Hazelgrove at last. "Congratulations!"

Honey leaped up in the air, her tail wiggling joyfully. "I did it!" she cheered.

"Well done!" her friends exclaimed, crowding round to hug her.

"You must learn the poem by heart, Honey," said Mr Hazelgrove.

"Yes, sir!" Honey replied excitedly. She couldn't wait to get started.

Chapter Three

"Only five days to the ball," Natalie said excitedly, as the friends walked to school.

"Five days!" exclaimed Honey. "I'll never be ready in time!"

"Honey, you've practised that poem every day," said Evie. "You know it inside out, back to front and upside down!"

"We all know it," Florence added. "And Mr Hazelgrove's been really pleased with you at rehearsals."

"But I still might mess it up," Honey said anxiously. "And everyone will be watching." She ran through the poem one more time.

"I hope we're rehearsing the dance again today," said Florence when Honey had finished. They'd been dancing almost every day at school.

"We're getting better and better," Evie said. "Even you, Nat!" she added, winking at Natalie.

Natalie giggled. "I'm not sure Albie would agree. I keep treading on his toes."

"Have you worked out what he and Harvey are up to yet, Honey?" asked Florence.

Honey shook her head. "I keep listening at their bedroom door, but I haven't heard them mention their 'fantastic trick'. All they do is complain about having to dance."

They all laughed.

"I'm picking strawberries after school," said Florence. "Do you want to come? We could have a scout around for Harvey and Albie at the same time."

"Good idea," they all agreed.

Straight after school, the friends collected baskets from Florence's burrow, then headed for the strawberry patch on the far side of the Stepping Stones. On the way, they spotted Mr Morningdew and Mr Pennyroyal in the distance. They were

hanging lanterns and strings of shiny berries along the path that led from Foxglove Hollow to the raft.

Bluebell Woods

There were plenty of ripe strawberries growing near the edge of the wood and they soon filled their baskets. "No sign of Harvey and Albie," Florence said. "If they were this side of the Babbling Brook we'd have spotted them crossing the Stepping Stones."

"Unless they used their raft," Natalie said. "But the woods seem pretty quiet over here."

As they crossed back over the Stepping Stones, the sound of pipe and drum music filled the air. "What's that music?" asked Honey.

Florence pricked up her long ears. "The reed pipe orchestra. It sounds as though they're in Foxglove Hollow."

They ran to see and found the musicians rehearsing.

"Lovely!" said Natalie dreamily.

The musicians struck up a new tune. "Our dance tune!" exclaimed Honey.

Setting down their baskets, the four friends formed a line and began to dance. "That was pretty good," said Evie when the music ended. "I only messed up a couple of steps."

"Me, too," Natalie said, astonished.

"Didn't we say you'd be fine?" Evie said, squeezing her paw.

Florence picked up her basket. "We should go. My mum will be wondering where her strawberries are."

They hurried out of Foxglove Hollow and across Primrose Meadow, where Monty and his two little sisters were gathering grass stems. "What are you doing, Monty?" Honey asked.

"Picking grasses to weave baskets,"

he replied. "To hold the food at the ball."

"Everyone's busy," Natalie said, as they ran on. "I love it when we all work together."

"Especially when there's something so exciting to look forward to at the end of it all!" added Honey.

Next day, the four friends went to Buttercup Stitchery to collect Evie's dress. The seamstress fetched it from the back room.

"It's beautiful!" Evie exclaimed, stroking the emerald-green silk. "Thank you, Mrs Buttercup!"

Honey watched wistfully as Evie held up the dress.

Suddenly, the door swung open and Albie and Harvey came in. "Have you got any scraps of silk to spare, please, Mrs Buttercup?" Albie asked.

Honey and her friends exchanged puzzled glances.

Mrs Buttercup showed them the bins full of offcuts. "Help yourselves," she said. The boys began to rummage through them.

"What do you want silk for?" Honey asked.

"None of your business," Albie muttered.

He and Harvey took an armful of silk each, then thanked Mrs Buttercup and scampered out.

"What are they up to now?" groaned Honey.

"Let's follow them," Florence suggested. "Can we pick up Evie's dress later, please, Mrs Buttercup?"

"Of course," the seamstress said.

The four friends darted out of her workshop and raced after the boys. They followed them into Bluebell Woods, keeping behind trees and under bushes so they wouldn't be spotted.

At last, Harvey and Albie came to a clearing. Pulling aside some leaves, they uncovered a large cage made of twigs.

"What's that for?" Florence whispered to her friends.

The friends crept closer. Harvey and
Albie began to tear the silk into triangles.
As Honey edged forward to see better,
Albie caught sight of her. "Honey alert!"
he shouted.

Gathering up the silk and picking up
the cage between them, the boys dashed off.

"After them!" cried Florence. She
darted away, then looked back as she
heard a loud sob. Tears were pouring down
Honey's cheeks.

"What's wrong?" asked Natalie gently,
putting her arm round Honey.

"I'm … worried … about the
… the ball," Honey sobbed.
"So many things could go
wrong. Harvey and Albie
… that cage … what if
they lock me in it?"

"We won't let them!" said Evie.

"And what if I forget the poem?" Honey wailed.

"You know it perfectly," Florence said.

"And … I know I'm making a fuss, but I wish I didn't have to wear Hattie's old dress," Honey sniffed. "It's such a horrible colour and…"

"It's not that bad," Natalie said.

Honey blew her nose. "You're right. I'm just being silly."

"Hang on," said Florence. "My dad dyes wool for blankets. He mixed up some blue dye before he went out this morning. Why don't we colour Honey's dress?"

"Do you think it would work?" said Honey, her eyes brightening.

"There's only one way to find out," said Florence.

They charged over to Hedge End to
fetch Honey's dress, then scurried across
Primrose Meadow to Florence's burrow.
There was nobody in and they went
straight to Mr Candytuft's workroom.
A half-knitted blanket was draped over a
chair and some wisps of sheep's wool lay
on the table. Beside the table stood a
bucket of blue dye.

"Here goes," said Honey, dropping the
dress into the bucket. Florence stirred it in
with a twig, then touched her tail three
times for luck.

"I hope it works," Natalie said.

They all stared into the bucket. "How long does it take, Florence?" asked Evie.

"I'm not sure," replied Florence. "But let's do some skipping while we wait."

Half an hour later, the friends gathered eagerly round the bucket of dye. Florence lifted the dress out and they all gasped in horror.

"It's ruined!" wailed Honey.

The dress was now bluey-grey with bright blue streaks and blotches.

"We could try rinsing it," suggested Natalie in a worried voice.

Florence dropped the dress into a bucket of clean water. The water turned blue, but when she lifted the dress out again, the streaks were still there.

Evie fetched a bar of soap and frantically rubbed it in. When they rinsed the dress again, it was as streaky as ever.

"It's a disaster!" Honey groaned. "And what am I going to tell my mum?"

Chapter
Four

"You've spoiled a perfectly good silk dress!" Mrs Pennyroyal said crossly, as she examined Honey's dress.

"I'm really sorry, Mum," said Honey, trying not to cry.

"It was my idea," Florence said, hanging her head.

"But we all went along with it," Evie added apologetically.

Mrs Pennyroyal sighed.

"Can I still go to the ball?" Honey sniffed.

"What you did was wrong," said Mrs Pennyroyal sternly. "But a ruined dress isn't the end of the world. Yes, you can still go to the ball, Honey. You'll just have to wear your party dress."

Honey nodded sadly. Her party dress was too short for a ball, but it couldn't be helped.

"If you like," Mrs Pennyroyal added, "we can ask Mrs Buttercup to make a new silk sash for it, and to edge the sleeves and hem in matching silk to make it look a bit more special."

Honey perked up a little. "Thanks, Mum," she whispered.

"Go round to Mrs Buttercup's now and choose the colour," said Mrs Pennyroyal. "And I'll just have to use the material from this spoiled dress to make silk bow ties for Dad and the boys."

The friends scampered away. "That wasn't as bad as I thought it would be," said Honey.

"I was worried she'd tell our mums and none of us would be allowed to go to the ball," said Evie.

"And you're going to have a pretty dress after all, Honey," Florence added. She still felt guilty for getting her friend into trouble, but at least things had turned out all right in the end.

There was only one length of silk left in Mrs Buttercup's workshop. It was ruby red and Honey knew it would look perfect against the pale pink of her party dress.

While she was admiring it, Jemima took the ruby silk and spread it out on the worktable. "What are you doing?" squeaked Honey, alarmed.

"Cutting out a dress," Jemima said. "It's our last order for the ball."

"What's the trouble?" asked Mrs Buttercup, coming over.

"Mum sent me to choose some silk to  edge my party dress," Honey explained.

"I'm sorry, Honey," said Mrs Buttercup, "but there's no silk left."

Honey was dismayed. "What am I going to do?"

"Where do you get your silk, Mrs Buttercup?" asked Florence.

"From Mr Brushtail, the weaver. He's a fox who lives on the far side of Bluebell Woods."

"We could buy some from him," Natalie suggested.

Mrs Buttercup frowned. "It's a long way."

"No problem," said Evie. "Can you give us directions, please?"

Mrs Buttercup quickly sketched a map. "There. I hope he can help you."

The four friends hurried outside and looked at the map.

"When can we go?" said Honey.

"Well, it's Saturday tomorrow, so maybe we can go then," said Evie.

"There's a dance rehearsal at four o'clock, though," Florence reminded her. "We'll have to be back for that."

The friends set off for Mr Brushtail's soon after dawn the next day. They took a picnic with them, and a foraging basket so they could gather food to exchange for the silk.

"I love exploring the woods!" Evie exclaimed, as they followed a narrow, winding path through the shady trees.

They hurried along, stopping now and then to check the map. "I hope it's not much further," Honey said. "I'm so excited I can't wait to get there."

At last, they reached a part of the woods where sunlight shone between the leaves of silver birch trees, dappling the ground. "This must be the birch copse," said Natalie. "So Mr Brushtail's den is somewhere around here."

"Next to a clump of foxgloves," said Evie, checking the map.

Honey climbed up on a fallen tree and looked round. "There!" she said, pointing.

They headed towards the foxgloves and found a large hole leading underground. "This must be it!" Honey squeaked, her whiskers twitching with anticipation.

"Hello," Florence called, knocking on the door. "Mr Brushtail, are you in?"

They heard movement down in the den, then a very old fox appeared. His orange fur was flecked with white. "I'm Mr Brushtail. Was someone looking for me?"

"Mrs Buttercup sent us," said Evie.

"To buy spider silk!" Honey burst out.

Mr Brushtail smiled. "Come in."

They followed him down the tunnel and came out in a dusty living room with a wooden loom in one corner. Honey's eyes brightened with excitement as Mr Brushtail opened a cupboard. Inside was a single length of pale pink silk.

"This is all I've got left, I'm afraid," he said. "It's not enough to make a dress." He shook the silk out and draped it across the table. "You should get a skirt out of it."

"It's to edge the hem and sleeves of my party dress," explained Honey, fingering the soft fabric. "And to make a sash."

"There's enough for that."

Florence put her basket on the table. "We've brought some cherries to exchange for the silk."

"My favourite!" cried Mr Brushtail. He tipped them into a bowl, then folded the silk and placed it in Florence's basket. "Please give my regards to Mrs Buttercup."

"We will," Honey said. "Thank you!"

The four friends ran up the tunnel into the sunshine. "Come on!" said Honey. "We've got to get to Mrs Buttercup's so she can start work on my dress. It's only three days to the ball."

Halfway home, they sat down to share their picnic. There were carrot pasties, sorrel and chickweed salad, strawberry cookies and elderflower cordial.

"Delicious!" Honey said, gobbling down a pasty.

"I helped my mum make them for the ball, but luckily there were a few left over," said Florence, helping herself to one. "What are you and your mum making, Nat?"

Natalie was staring at the ground, her eyes thoughtful.

"Nat?" said Evie. She touched Natalie's arm.

"Oh, sorry," Natalie said, looking up. "I've had an idea. I know how you can have a new dress for the ball, Honey."

"How?" Honey squeaked.

"You remember all those offcuts in Mrs Buttercup's bins? If we cut out some diamond shapes and sew them together, we'll have a length of multi-coloured silk."

"Like patchwork?" Evie asked.

"Yes," agreed Natalie. "So the top of Honey's dress could be made out of silk patchwork and the skirt could be made from Mr Brushtail's pink silk."

"Brilliant!" Florence and Evie exclaimed.

"Don't just sit here!" Honey gasped. "Eat up quickly so we can get to Mrs Buttercup's."

Chapter Five

The four friends were nearly home when they came upon Harvey and Albie with their cage. It was resting on a low stage and Albie was inside, tying silk bunting to the wooden bars. "That's why they wanted the silk," Florence whispered. "To make bunting. I wonder why…"

"I don't even want to think about Harvey and Albie right now," said Honey. "We need to get to Mrs Buttercup's."

They ran on through the woods, then across Primrose Meadow to Buttercup

Stitchery. "Did Mr Brushtail have any silk?" Mrs Buttercup asked.

"Yes. He sent his regards," Honey panted. "And we've had a brilliant idea!" She told Mrs Buttercup Natalie's suggestion.

"I'm sure that would work," said Mrs Buttercup, frowning. "I just don't know if we've got time."

Honey's face fell. "I'll fetch my party dress then," she said sadly.

"What if we all help?" said Evie. "We've got a bit of time before our dance rehearsal."

"Right, let's get cracking." Mrs Buttercup fetched the pattern book and Honey leafed through it quickly.

"I saw the perfect one when Evie was choosing hers," she said. She flipped over a few more pages. "Here, look!" Honey pointed to the high-waisted dress with the full skirt that she'd admired before.

"That will suit you very well," said Mrs Buttercup. "Let's take your measurements." Raising her voice, she called to Jemima, "Will you make a start on Honey's skirt?"

Jemima came out of the back room. "Here's the silk for the skirt," said Florence, handing it over. "And this is the pattern Honey's chosen."

Jemima spread out the pink silk on the table and began to cut.

Florence, Natalie and Evie delved in the bins at the back of the workroom.

"This silk's gorgeous," said Evie. "It's terrible to think of it being thrown away."

"Perhaps we could make some bunting for the ball with the leftovers," suggested Natalie. "It looked good on Harvey and Albie's cage."

It didn't take long for the friends to find plenty of colourful offcuts. They spread them on the table. "I'll cut them out," said Evie, picking up some scissors. "And you two can start sewing them together."

"Three," said Honey, running over. "Mrs Buttercup's finished measuring me so I can help, too."

The reed pipe orchestra was waiting in
Foxglove Hollow when the four friends
arrived for the rehearsal.

"Made it!" said Natalie breathlessly.

"Sewing those diamonds together took
ages," Florence said. "Still, it's done now
and—"

"And my dress will be ready on the
morning of the ball!" Honey cut in.
"Thanks for all your help."

Mr Hazelgrove and Mrs Wintergreen
arrived. "Line up, everyone," called Mrs
Wintergreen.

When the dancers were ready, the
musicians started to play and the girls
skipped forward – one, two, three, four.
The boys skipped after them, then came
the twirls, side skips and jumps.

Bluebell Woods

As they turned to their partners, Mrs Wintergreen clapped her paws. "Stop! Some of you are missing the beat."

"That's me," whispered Natalie.

"And some are forgetting the steps."

"That's me, too," Natalie sighed.

"You'll soon pick it up again," said Florence. "You were great yesterday."

The dance started once more. This time Natalie remembered the steps.

"Well done!" Mrs Wintergreen called out, as the girls turned towards their partners.

Twirling this way and that, they danced right round Foxglove Hollow with their partners. "Now form a double line for the Grand Procession," called Mr Hazelgrove, as the music ended.

"That wasn't bad," said Evie, helping Natalie steer Albie into the line behind Hattie and Harvey, who were right at the front.

"I only missed a couple of steps," Natalie said, smiling with relief.

"You didn't miss my feet, though," complained Albie, rubbing his toes.

"Sorry," Natalie apologized. "I'm trying my best, honestly."

Honey and Monty then joined the line

behind them. "It'll look fantastic when we're all wearing our ball dresses," said Honey.

Florence and Luke were the last to join the line. "Link arms with your partner and follow me," called Mr Hazelgrove. "This is the route for the Grand Procession."

They followed him around the outside of Foxglove Hollow, then along the path that led to the raft. *Only three more days to go!* Honey thought excitedly.

Chapter
Six

For the next two days, Bluebell Woods
was a hive of activity. Honey, Florence,
Evie, Natalie and the other youngsters
went foraging for berries, roots and leaves.
The village was filled with delicious smells
as rabbits, weasels and hedgehogs turned
them into mouth-watering treats for the
ball feast. The mice and squirrels were
busy, too, decorating trees and bushes with
strings of painted seeds and glossy berries.

When they weren't gathering baskets
of cherries and mushrooms, or helping

with the baking, the four friends worked on their bunting. They cut the silk into triangles, hemmed them neatly, then sewed them to long honeysuckle stems.

"This will be perfect," said Mrs Pennyroyal. "Well done, girls."

Midsummer's Day arrived at last. Honey woke early and sprang out of bed. She raced round to Buttercup Stitchery without even stopping for breakfast. The seamstress was opening her shutters when she arrived.

"Is it finished?" panted Honey.

Smiling, Mrs Buttercup fetched the dress from the back room.

"It's gorgeous!" Honey gasped. The colourful dress gleamed in the early morning sun that slanted through the windows.

"Try it on," said Mrs Buttercup.

Honey changed quickly, then gazed at her reflection in the mirror. "Thank you so much," she said.

The door opened and Mrs Pennyroyal came in with a basket over her arm. She stopped dead. "Honey, you look beautiful!" she exclaimed.

"Thanks, Mum." Honey hugged her. "I'm the luckiest mouse in the whole of Bluebell Woods."

Mrs Pennyroyal smiled at Mrs Buttercup. "I've brought you some walnuts, Mrs Buttercup, to pay for the alterations to Honey's party dress, but I'll have to bring something else as well. It must have taken ages to make it." She handed the basket to the seamstress.

"These nuts will be fine," Mrs Buttercup said. "Honey and her friends helped with the sewing."

Honey hid the dress in her wardrobe as soon as she and her mum got home. She didn't want anyone else to see it before the ball.

"Can I help with anything, Mum?" she asked, going into the kitchen where Hattie was icing some cherry buns.

"There's all this food to be put into baskets," her mum said, waving a paw at the kitchen table, which was full of treats for the feast.

"And don't eat any of it!" said Hattie, laughing.

As Honey went to fetch a basket, she heard a loud rumbling outside. Running out to see what it was, she found Mr Wintergreen with his handcart, which was piled high with baskets. Monty was with him, helping to steer.

"Steady now, Monty," Mr Wintergreen said. "Mind that tree root or this lot'll go over. Oh, hello, Honey." The cart came to a halt as he spotted the young mouse. "I'm collecting food to take across to Midsummer Island," said Mr Wintergreen.

"I'll bring it out," Honey said. She darted inside. "Mr Wintergreen and Monty are here for the food, Mum."

Bluebell Woods

Hattie had finished icing the buns and she packed the baskets while Honey carried them outside. Mrs Pennyroyal came out with a list, and she and Mr Wintergreen ticked things off together while Honey and Monty loaded the food on to the cart.

"Is this all for tonight?" Honey asked, staring at the mountain of baskets.

"Yes," said Mr Wintergreen. "And more besides. There are still a few calls to make."

When Mr Wintergreen and Monty
had gone, Honey decided to practise
the poem, even though she'd rehearsed
it at least a hundred times. She closed
her bedroom door and cleared her throat.
"Midsummer's Day, a special day,"
she began.

As she started the second line, she
heard a squeaky voice outside her door.

> *"Midsummer's Day, when girlies play*
> *And dress up all in pink.*
> *They think they're sweet,*
> *but mind their feet –*
> *They really, really stink!"*

Throwing open her door, Honey found
Harvey and Albie outside.

"Stop it!" she cried. "You'll make me
forget the proper words."

Her brothers scurried away, laughing.

Bluebell Woods

Evening came at last. Honey scampered to her bedroom and took out her new dress. With trembling paws, she pulled it on and fastened the buttons. When she went into the kitchen, Hattie gasped. "You look amazing!"

Mr Pennyroyal stared at her, open-mouthed. "You do," he said, hugging her.

Harvey and Albie came in, complaining loudly about too-tight collars and waistbands. They fell silent when they saw Honey. "Whoa, Honey, I nearly didn't recognize you," Harvey said, at last.

Honey smiled. For the first time ever, Harvey had said something that was almost complimentary.

The sun was low in the sky as the Pennyroyals came out from under the hedgerow, and the air was already cooling after the heat of the day. They walked to Foxglove Hollow, and Honey stopped on the ridge and gazed spellbound at everyone and everything. Down below, the orchestra were tuning their instruments, and her brightly dressed friends and neighbours were chatting and laughing. Mr Hazelgrove, in a rather tight, red silk suit, was trying to gather all the dancers together.

"Told you it would be good," said Hattie.

"It's better than good," whispered Honey. "It's fantastic!"

Hattie spotted her friend Tamsin in the crowd and ran down to speak to her.

"Come on, Harvey. Mustn't be late!" Albie cried.

He and Harvey dashed off down the
slope.

"Can I go now, too, Mum?" Honey
asked.

"Of course," her mum replied. "Good
luck with the poem and the dance,
darling."

"Thanks." Honey sped down the slope
after her brothers. She caught them up
near the bottom. "That trick of yours," she
panted. "You're not still doing it tonight,
are you?"

"Might be," said Harvey, winking at her.

"Harvey…" Honey began. But they'd already run off. She stared after them, dismayed, wishing she knew what they were up to. What if they made her forget the poem? Or perhaps they were planning to ruin the dance somehow. She wanted this to be an evening to remember, but she wanted to remember it for all the right reasons!

Chapter Seven

Honey spotted Florence, Evie and Natalie waving and, pushing her fears to the back of her mind, she ran over to join them.

"Wow!" they said together, admiring her dress.

"I'm over the moon." Honey twirled round. "And I wouldn't have got this amazing dress if it wasn't for you." She smiled at her friends. "You all look great."

"I made these for us," Natalie said shyly. She held out necklaces made from dog rose petals and speedwell flowers.

"They're gorgeous, Nat," said Evie.

They put them on and Florence sniffed the rose petals. "We won't just look good, we'll smell good, too!" She laughed.

Mr Hazelgrove bustled over. "Ready, Honey?" he asked.

"Yes, sir."

As Mr Hazelgrove hurried off, Honey turned to her friends. "I can't remember the first line," she gasped, panic-stricken.

"Of course you do!" said Evie.

"Midsummer's Day, when girlies play and dress up all in pink…" began Honey. "No, that's Harvey and Albie's version!" She looked at her friends in horror. "I'm going to mess it up, I know I am."

"You'll be fine," Florence reassured her. "You've been brilliant in rehearsals."

"I can't do it," cried Honey.

Florence, Evie and Natalie exchanged anxious glances. "Of course you can do it, Honey," said Evie. "You're a born performer."

"You'll be great," Natalie said, squeezing her paw. "Honestly, Honey, you're worrying about nothing."

"Friends," called Mr Hazelgrove in his loudest voice. He stood on the tree-stump stage, halfway up the slope. "To begin the festivities, Honey Pennyroyal will recite our traditional Midsummer Poem."

"What am I going to do?" wailed Honey.

"'Midsummer's Day, a special day…'
That's the first line," said Florence.

"And the title's 'Midsummer'," Evie
reminded her. "Don't forget to say what
it's called."

"Yes, yes. I think I remember it now,"
Honey said. She gave her friends an
agonized glance, then clambered on to the
stage to join Mr Hazelgrove.

"Poor thing," said Natalie. "I hope she
gets it right."

Honey stood beside the teacher.
Everyone was watching her. Her gaze
swept over her friends and family in their
smart dresses and suits. They all expected
her to give a great performance; she
couldn't let them down. Suddenly, she
spotted Harvey and Albie and looked
away quickly, afraid that they'd make her

forget the words again. She turned towards her friends. *Midsummer*, Florence mouthed at her.

Honey took a deep, shaky breath. "Midsummer," she quavered. Suddenly, she felt a rush of fierce determination to succeed. "Midsummer," she said, more confidently.

"Midsummer's Day, a special day
Of joy and jubilation.
Come to the ball. Come one, come all,
And join the celebration!
For winter's snowy cold has fled
And summer's warmth is here;
The woods are sweet with birdsong
And our hearts are full of cheer.
There's tasty food a-plenty:
Berries, leaves and scented flowers.
In dappled glades or sunny spots
We while away the hours.

Bluebell Woods

Now Primrose Meadow's lush and green;
The Babbling Brook glides by;
The trees wear summer finery,
And overhead the sky
Is azure blue and cloudless
And, of course, we all agree
That Bluebell Woods, our Bluebell Woods,
Is the perfect place to be!"

There was a moment of total stillness when she'd finished, then everyone applauded. "Bravo, Honey!" someone called. Honey held out her silk skirt and curtseyed, then hurried down the slope to where her classmates were lining up for the dance. *I did it,* she thought proudly. *I really did it!*

"Well done, Honey," Florence said when Honey joined them. "We could hear you perfectly."

"Thanks," replied Honey. "I enjoyed it in the end."

The dancers were ready and the orchestra had finished tuning up. "Wish me luck," whispered Natalie, as they waited for the music to start. The sky was darkening along its eastern edge and the candle lanterns were beginning to twinkle.

"You won't need luck," said Evie. "You'll be fine."

The orchestra struck up and the girls skipped forward, keeping in time with the beat of Mr Wintergreen's drum. The boys skipped up behind them, their feet setting the grass rustling. Then they were into their twirls and side skips. Honey glanced at Natalie and smiled, glad to see that her friend seemed to be having fun.

The dance ended to more applause. As the young animals lined up for the Grand Procession, Honey noticed that darkness was spreading right across the sky. Now the lanterns shone out more strongly, setting the strings of berries gleaming.

Mr Hazelgrove led the Grand Procession. Round Foxglove Hollow they walked, then along the path leading to the

Babbling Brook. Honey saw Natalie's mum
and dad join on behind them. Her parents
were with them, and Evie's and Florence's
weren't far behind.

The path to the raft was lit by
flickering candlelight that created
deliciously mysterious shadows.

"I'm so excited," whispered Honey,
as they spotted Mr Willowherb ahead,
waiting on his raft. It was decked with
colourful flowers and sprays of leaves.

"Me, too," Monty replied in a low
voice. "My mum's made damson jellies
and I can't wait to try one."

The youngsters crowded on to the raft.
The four friends watched eagerly as they
neared Midsummer Island.

"Look at all the lights and decorations,"
said Natalie in an awed voice.

Honey could hardly wait to land. *What
a night this is going to be*, she thought.

Chapter Eight

The friends held up their dresses as Mr Willowherb helped them ashore; they didn't want to get them wet.

"Let's explore," said Evie. She led the way towards a wide clearing that had been set up for dancing, with chairs and tables on three sides. On the fourth side were long trestle tables piled high with every type of food. Lanterns flickered all around.

"There's our bunting!" cried Florence, spotting their colourful flags fluttering above the tables of food.

Bluebell Woods

The raft came back to the island with more guests, including Honey's parents.

"The poem was excellent," said Mr Pennyroyal. "Well done, Honey."

"Thanks," Honey said, beaming. "Has anyone seen Albie and Harvey?" she asked, when her parents had gone. "I'm still worried about their 'fantastic trick'."

"They're over there," Evie said, pointing. The boys were sneaking cookies from the end of one of the tables.

"We're safe for a bit then," said Honey, relieved. "Harvey and Albie never let anything get in the way of eating."

When everyone had crossed to Midsummer Island, the orchestra began to play a jig. "Let's dance!" Florence cried.

"I'll watch for a bit, thanks," said Natalie.

"Oh no, Nat, you have to join in," said Evie. She and Florence grabbed Natalie's arms and pulled her on to the dance floor.

They jigged merrily, linking paws and whirling each other round in time to the music.

"This is so much fun!" Honey panted.

They danced until the orchestra stopped for a break. "Supper is served," announced Mr Hazelgrove.

The four friends queued up eagerly, the music still ringing in their ears and their feet itching to dance again.

"Look at all this!" Natalie exclaimed as they reached the table. There were pies and pasties, jellies, cookies, cakes and buns.

They helped themselves to a little bit
of everything and came away from the
buffet with loaded plates. They sat at an
empty table next to the dance floor.

"Delicious!" announced Honey, biting
into a mushroom tart.

Honey's parents were sitting across
the dance floor from them, fanning
themselves with horse chestnut leaves.

"They look hot," said Florence.

"No wonder. Did you see them

dancing?" Honey said. "They even attempted the jig. And my dad's dancing is soooo embarrassing!"

They all laughed.

When they'd finished eating, Mr Hazelgrove came out into the middle of the dance floor. "Friends," he said, "two of my pupils have prepared some special entertainment for you. They have worked on this by themselves and showed it to Mrs Wintergreen and myself only two days ago. We're sure you will enjoy it."

Albie and Harvey appeared from behind the buffet tables. They were dressed as magicians, in long cloaks covered with stars and moons. Albie's cloak was red and Harvey's was blue.

"We're going to show you our fantastic trick," Harvey announced.

"Oh no," Honey groaned. She watched nervously as the twins carried their low stage to the middle of the dance floor, then fetched their bunting-draped cage and set it on top. "I suppose they brought that stuff over on their raft," she added.

Albie climbed into the cage and Harvey shut the door. He covered the cage with a black cloth. "Abracadabra!" He pointed his front paws at the cage, then whisked the cloth off. The cage was empty; Albie had vanished.

The audience clapped and cheered.

"How did he do that?" gasped Natalie.

"I don't know," Honey said. "But let's hope he can't bring Albie back!"

Harvey covered the cage again. "Now to make him reappear," he said. "Abracadabra!" As he yanked the cloth aside, they saw Albie sitting in the cage, grinning. Now he was wearing a blue cloak, the same as Harvey's.

"That really was a fantastic trick!" said Evie, clapping enthusiastically.

Honey nodded. "Talent must run in the family... At least this time they weren't playing a trick on me. But I still don't trust them an inch!"

The orchestra struck up again and they jigged and whirled, swept along by the rhythm and the excitement.

All too soon, Mr Hazelgrove announced the last dance. "What a shame," sighed Natalie.

"It's not over yet," said Honey. The orchestra began to play and the friends linked arms and launched themselves into an energetic dance, kicking their legs high and spinning round and round. As the music ended, they collapsed in a giggling heap.

"What a brilliant night!" Evie said, wriggling out from underneath Florence.

"It was," they all agreed.

"The best night of our lives!" exclaimed Natalie.

Honey sighed happily. "I don't know about you, but I can't wait for next year!"

Have you read?

Bluebell Woods

Liss Norton

Florence's Birthday Wish